The Story of the Invention of Steel Pens

Henry Bore

Contents

THE STORY OF THE INVENTION OF STEEL PENS

BY

Henry Bore

In these days of Public Schools and extended facilities for popular education it would be difficult to find many people unaccustomed to the use of steel pens, but although the manufacture of this article by presses and tools must have been introduced during the first quarter of the present century, the inquirer after knowledge would scarcely find a dozen persons who could give any definite information as to when, where, and by whom this invention was made. Less than two decades ago there were three men living who could have answered this question, but two of them passed away without making any sign, and the third--Sir Josiah Mason--has left on record that his friend and patron--Mr. Samuel Harrison--about the year 1780, made a steel pen for Dr. Priestley.

This interesting fact does not contribute anything toward solving the question, Who was the first manufacturer of steel pens by mechanical appliances? In the absence of any definite information, the balance of testimony tends to prove that steel pens were first made by tools, worked by a screw press, about the beginning of the third decade of the present century, and the names associated with their manufacture were John Mitchell, Joseph Gillott, and Josiah Mason, each, in his own way, doing something toward perfecting the manufacture by mechanical means.

The earliest references to pens are probably those in the Bible, and are to be found in Judges v. 14, 1st Kings xxi. 8, Job xix. 24, Psalm xlv. 1., Isaiah viii. 1, Jeremiah viii. 8 and xvii. 1. But these chiefly refer to the iron stylus, though the first in Jeremiah--taken in reference to the mention of a penknife, xxxvi. 23--would seem to imply that a reed was in use at that period.

There is a reference to "pen and ink" in the 3d Epistle of John xiii. 5, which was written about A.D. 85, and as pens made in brass and silver were used in the Greek and Roman Empires at that time, it is probable that a metallic pen or reed was alluded to.

Pens and reeds made in the precious metals and bronze appear to have been in use at the commencement of the present era. The following are a few notable instances:

"The Queen of Hungary, in the year 1540, had a silver pen bestowed upon her, which had this inscription upon it: *'Publii Ovidii Calamus,'* found under the ruins of some monument in that country, as Mr. Sands, in the Life of Ovid (prefixed to his Metamorphosis) relates. -- *"Humane Industry; or, a History of Mechanical Arts," by Thos. Powell, D.D.: London, 1661, page 61.*"

This was probably a silver reed, and, from the locality in which it was found, was once the property of the poet Ovid. Publius Ovidius Naso was born in the year 43 B.C., and died 18 A.D. He was exiled at the age of 30 to Tomi, a town south of the delta of the Danube. This at present is in modern Bulgaria, but at the period mentioned was in the ancient kingdom of Hungary.

From "Notes and Queries," in Birmingham *Weekly Post*, we take the following:

"EARLY METALLIC PENS.---Metallic pens are generally supposed to have been unknown before the early part of the last century, when gold and silver pens are occasionally referred to as novel luxuries. I have, however, recently found a description and an engraving of one found in excavating Pompeii, and which is now preserved in the Museum at Naples. It is described in the quarto volume 'Les Monuments du Musee National de Naples, graves sur cuivre par les meillures artistes Italienes. Texte par Domenico Monaco, Conservateur du meme Musee,

Naples, 1882,' and is in the Catalogue:

"' Plate I26 (v) Plume en bronze, taillee parfaitement a la facon de nos plumes 0.13 cent.

"' Plate I26 (y) Plume en roseau [reed] trouvee pres d'un papyrus a Herculaneum.'

"The former (v) is engraved to look like an ordinary reed pen, as now used universally in the East; and the other (y) has a spear shape, or almond shape (like many modern metallic pens), but with a sort of fillet or ring on the stem, which indicates that the 'y' example is not a reed, but a metallic stylus, or pen, while the 'v' example is shown clearly as a 'reed.' The two are, however, certainly older than A.D. 79, when Pompeii and Herculaneum were buried by the eruption of Vesuvius."

According to Father Montfaucon, the patriarchs of Constantinople, under the Greek Empire, were accustomed to sign their allocutions with tubular pens of silver, similar in shape to the reed pens which are still used by Oriental nations.

The following are translated from the French "Notes and Queries "-- L'Intermediare:

"A METALLIC PEN IN THE FOURTEENTH CENTURY.--M. Reni de Bellwal, in a very learned volume which he has published recently, on the first campaign of Edward III. in France, says (p. 95) with respect to the fictitious pieces (documents) fabricated by Robert d'Artois, that a clerk of Jeanne wrote the deeds, and made use of a bronze pen to enable him the better to disguise his writing. This plainly refers to a pen, and not to a stylus. Is there any record of the use of metallic pens at any period anterior to the fourteenth century? It is very satisfactory, however, to establish (as the French used to say) 'les preuves de 1300.'"--L'Intermediare.

In the *Vieux-Neuf* of M. Ed. Fournier (vol. ii., p. 22, note) there is mentioned--according to the documents used in the prosecution of Robert d'Artois, which are in the Archives--'the bronze pen' with which the forgers in the pay of the count wrote the false papers which he required. M. Fournier also quotes from 'Montfaucon' 'the silver reeds' with which the Constantinople patriarchs used to write their letters."-- CUTHBERT, *L'Intermediare,* 1st June, 1864.

"METALLIC PENS (XV., 68).-Writing was done in the Middle Ages sometimes with a metal *stylus,* or perhaps with a metal pen; with the former on wax, and with the pen on parchment or vellum. 'At Trinity College, Cambridge, is a manuscript illustration of Eadwine, a monk of Canterbury, and at the end the writer is represented with a metal pen in his hand.' (See Bibliomania in the Middle Ages, p. 103). I have in my possession a metal pen of Dutch manufacture, dating certainly from the year 1717, mounted on the same pencilholder, with a piece of solid plumbago, in a memorandum book of the same year."--SAM: TIMMINS.

"Mr. Le Chauvine Gal, Prior of the collegiate of St. Peter and St. Bars at Aosta, had in his collection of Roman antiquities a bronze pen, slit, found in a tomb, among a number of lamps and lachrymatory vases. M. Aubert has given a drawing and description of it in a work on Aosta. It was subsequently stolen from him by a collector."--- CHAMBERY, Un Savoyard, *L'Intermediare,* 25th May, 1868.

"METALLIC PENS,--In a precious volume (an account of the books of the Decretalia) preserved in the library of Saint Antoine, of Padua, the following notice is to be found at the bottom of the last page: 'This work is fashioned and by diligence finished for the service of God, not with ink of quill nor with brazen reed, but with a certain invention of printing or reproducing by John Fust, citizen of Mayence, and Peter Schoeiffer, of Gernsheim, Dec. 17th, 1465, A.D.' Here, then, we have a document proving the existence of metallic pens in the Middle Ages. But has any such pen come down to us? If so, could a detailed description of it be obtained? On the other hand, I am curious to know if it is possible that platinum was used in the eighteenth century in the manufacture of pens, or whether it is necessary to attribute a peculiar meaning to the 'platinum pen' in the following passage of the system of shorthand by Bertin (edit. of the year iv., p. 93) (1793). 'Those of steel and platinum are most convenient; these latter have the advantage of all others, in that they hold the ink a long time, and run over the paper easily, and are not liable to corrosion by any simple acid.' I am ignorant of what the same author means when he mentions the endless pen, which would certainly be the best. "--J. CAMUS, *L'Intermediare.*

"Metallic pens were used before the fifteenth century; they were in use at the court of Augustus." See *L'Intermed.* (I. 69, 94, 141; II. 319.) Consult also *Le Vieux-Neuf* Ed. Fournier.--A.D.

The following extracts show there have been several claimants, on the Continent, who profess to have invented metallic pens, made from steel, in the early part of the eighteenth century; but the reader had better suspend his judgment until he has read the notes that follow them:

"A manuscript, entitled 'Historical Chronicle of Aix-la-Chapelle, second book, 1748,' places on record the claims of Johann Janssen, a magistrate of that place, as the inventor of steel pens. 'Just at the meeting of the congress [after the Austrian war] I may without boasting, claim the honour of having invented a new pen. It is, perhaps, not an accident that God should have inspired me at the present time with the idea of making steel pens, for all the envoys here assembled have bought the first that have been made; therewith, as may be hoped, to sign a treaty of peace, which, with God's blessing, shall be as permanent as the hard steel with which it is written. Of these pens, as I have invented them, no man hath before seen or heard. If kept clean and free from rust and ink, they will continue fit for use for many years. Indeed, a man may write twenty reams of paper with one, and the last line would be written as well as the first. They are now sent into every corner of the world as a rare thing--to Spain, France, England and Holland. Others will no doubt make imitations of my pens, but I am the man who first invented and made them. I have sold a great number of them at home and abroad at 1s. each, and I dispose of them as quickly as I can make them.'"

In an article on Writing Instruments, which appeared in the Berlin *Paper Zeitung,* on the 19th of May, 1887, the author says:

"A school teacher of Koningberg, named Burger, in the year 1808, made pens from metal, but he got poor by his trials. After this time, and probably imitating the pens of Burger, the English began to take in hand the manufacture of pens; *especially Perry,* he having perfected the pens, as he did not restrict himself to the simple straight slit, but he made cuts in the sides of different kinds."

In a pamphlet upon the manufacture of steel pens, published in Paris, in 1884, the writer says:

"The invention of the metallic pen is due to a French mechanic--Arnoux--who lived in the eighteenth century, who made as far back as 1750 a number of metallic pens as a curiosity. This invention did not have any immediate result in France but spread to England, and became in Birmingham, about 1830, a very prosperous industry. A very curious fact about this trade is that, in England, it does not exist out of Birmingham, where there are about ten manufactories. In France it has become localized in Boulogne."

There is also the "nameless Sheffield Artisan," who so frequently figures in newspaper paragraphs as the inventor of steel pens; and William Gadsby, a mathematical instrument maker, who for his own use constructed a clumsy article from the mainspring of a watch; but it is not till the beginning of the eighteenth century that we get anything authentic respecting the making of metallic pens. "Este," writing in "Local Notes and Queries" (Birmingham Weekly Post) *mentions a remarkable little volume supplied to the members of the States General of Holland, in the possession of Mr. W. Bragge, of Sheffield, dated 1717. It contained a silver pencil case, in two parts, one holding a piece of plumbago, mounted like a crayon, and the other a* metallic pen. We have seen this unique book (now the property of Mr. Sam: Timmins). The pen is of the barrel shape, apparently silver, and it must be regarded as the earliest authentic metallic pen. Of the date there can be no doubt, as the pen is made to pass through loops in the cover of the volume to keep it closed, after the manner of pocket books, and the book bears the date, printed on the title page, 1717.

Pope, about the same time, received from Lady Frances Shirley a present of a standish, containing a STEEL and a gold pen. In acknowledging the receipt of this present, the poet wrote an ode, in which the following lines occur:

"Take at this hand celestial arms; Secure the radiant weapons wield; This *golden* lance shall guard desert, And, if a vice dares keep the field, This *steel* shall stab it to the heart. Awed, on my bended knees I fell, Received the weapons of the sky, And dipped them in the sable well-- The fount of fame or infamy. What well? What weapon? Flavia cries, A standish, *steel and golden pen!* It came from *Bertrand's,* * not the skies, I gave it you to write again."

*Bertrand kept a fancy shop in Bath. He died in 1755. His wife is mentioned by Horace Walpole, in his letter to George Montague, May 18th, 1749, which letter is printed in his Correspondence.

In No. 503 of the *Spectator,* bearing the date of October 7, 1712, Steele, mentioning the conspicuous manner in which a certain lady conducted herself in church, says:

"For she fixed her eyes upon the preacher, and as he said anything she approved, with one of Charles Mather's fine tablets, she set down the sentence, at once showing her fine hand, the *gold pen,* her readiness in writing, and her judgments in choosing what to write."

Edmund Waller, about the middle of the seventeenth century, acknowledged the receipt of a *silver pen* from a lady, in the following verses:

> "Madam! intending to have try'd,
> The silver favour which you gave,
> In ink the shining point I dy'd,
> And drench'd it in the sable wave
> When, grieved to be so foully stained,
> On you it thus to me complained.
>
> So I, the wronged pen to please,
> Made it my humble thanks express
> Unto your Ladyship, in these,
> And now 'tis forced to confess
> That your great self did ne'er indite
> Nor that to me more noble write."

Mr. G. A. Lomas, writing to the *Scientific American,* November 23, 1878, says:

"I write to inquire if you can give me information concerning the manufacture of metal pens in this country. I may be vain in the supposition, but I am persuaded that my people--the Shakers--were the originators of metal pens. I write this to you with a silver pen, one slit, that was made in the year 1819, at this village, by the Shakers. Two or three years previously to the use of silver pens, our people used brass plates for their manufacture, but soon found silver preferable. Some people sold these pens in the year 1819, at this village, for twenty-five cents, and disposed of all that could be made."

The writer further says the metal was made from silver coins.

This communication called forth the following from another correspondent:

"The letter in the *Scientific American,* November 23, 1878, with regard to the early manufacture of steel pens, reminds me of the following note which appeared in the *Boston Mechanic,* for August, 1835. 'The inventor of steel pens,' says the *Journal of Commerce,* was an American and a well-known resident of our city (New York), Mr. Peregrine Williamson. In the year 1800, Mr.W., then a working jeweler, at Baltimore, while attending an evening school, finding some difficulty in making a quill pen to suit him, made one of steel. It would not write well, however, for want of flexibility. After a while he made an additional slit on each side of the main one, and the pens were so much improved that Mr. W. was called to make them in such numbers as to eventually occupy his whole time, and that of a journeyman. At first the business was very profitable and enabled Mr. W. to realize for the labor of himself and journeyman a clear profit of six hundred dollars per month. The English soon borrowed the invention, and some who first engaged in the business realized immense fortunes.'"

We do not know how much reliance may be placed upon this statement, but, if the last assertion "that those who first engaged in the business realized immense fortunes" may be taken as a test, the whole must be received with a grain of salt. The letter appeared in the *Boston Mechanic,* in 1835, and at that date there were penmakers who had made a modest competence, but in no case were they possessed of immense fortunes.

In London *Notes and Queries,* the following appears respecting early steel pens:

"THE FIRST STEEL PEN.--(5th S., iii., 395.) Ten years before Dr. Priestley was born steel pens were in use. There are references to them in the Diary of John Byrom, who required them when writing shorthand. In a letter to his sister Phoebe, dated August, 1723, he mentions them as follows: 'Alas! alas! I cannot meet with a steel pen, no manner of where I believe I have asked at 375 places, but that which I have is at your service, as the owner himself always is.'" (Remains, Vol. i., 39.)

Mr. Ralph N. James, writing to *Notes and Queries,* gives the following extract from the very amusing "journey to Paris," by Dr. Martin Lister, 1698:

"There was one thing very curious, and that was a *Writing Instrument* of thick and strong silver wire, bound up like a hollow button or screw, with both ends pointing one way, and at a distance, so that a man might easily put his forefinger betwixt the two points, and the point divided in two, just like *our steel pens."-- London Notes and Queries,* vol. iii., page 346.

This note caused another writer, Mr. C.A. Ward, to send the following:

"STEEL PENS.--The extract given from Dr. M. Lister's, by Mr. Ralph N. James, is very interesting. The doctor there speaks of *'our steel pens,'* as if they were not at all uncommon. When the poet Churchill's effects were sold up, after his death, Nov. 10, 1764, they fetched extravagant prices; 'a common steel pen' brought L.5." -- *London Notes and Queries,* vol iii., page 474.

The following extract from **London Notes and Queries** gives very plausible reasons against placing confidence in the preceding and other notices of ancient steel pens:

"STEEL PENS. (5th S., vol. iii., pp. 346, 474.) May I ask whether, in giving the interesting references to the use of *steel pens* before the time of Priestley (one reference even going so far back as the seventeenth century) your correspondents have carefully considered what is meant by the terms. For my own part (of course I maybe quite wrong) I should naturally have anticipated *steel pens* in these references to mean not the modern steel nib for ordinary penmanship, but the ancient steel pen for drawing lines or ruling circles, such as is contained in every box of mathematical instruments. This would explain (to some extent) the great price fetched for a good one of Churchill's; a mere old steel nib would scarcely enter into a sale at all. It would explain, too, why a special process of hardening should be applied to a quill, in order to make it do duty for the steel instrument. One would scarcely think of hardening a quill in order to enable it to compete with a steel nib in some of the least desirable qualities, though one often wishes one could accomplish the reverse process, and soften or supple a steel 'stick frog,' so as to give it the elasticity of the grey goose quill. "--V. H. I. L. L. C. IV. (iv., 37, 5th S., **London Notes and Queries.**)

Mr. R. Prosser, author of "Birmingham Inventors and Inventions," in writing to the compiler of this work, says:

"It has often occurred to me that some of the very early references to metallic pens may perhaps mean the draughtsman's 'ruling pen,' and not an instrument made after the fashion of a quill pen with a slit in it. That it is possible to write with such an instrument this paragraph will show, but I must admit that it is not equal to one of Perry's J's."

From an entry in "Pepys' Diary," October 24, 1660, **drawing pens** appear to have been in use in London, at the time of the Restoration:

"To Mr. Lilly's, where, not finding Mr. Spong, I went to Mr. Greatorex, where I met him, and where I bought a **drawing pen.**"

In London **Notes and Queries** (4th S., xi., 440), the Rev. E. Smedley, editor of the **Encyclopoedia Metropolitana,** writing to his friend, Mr. H. Hawkins, April 10, 1833, says:

"The process of nibbing and shaving is one which I always abominated, and for years past I have taken refuge under the **Perryian** pens. The one with which I now write has been in use daily, and all day long, for more than a fortnight, and I consider that it still owes me quite as much worth as it has already furnished. Every packet contains nine pens, and on an average two out of that number fail to suit my hand, but the remaining seven are faithful servants, and their price is 2s."

In **London Notes and Queries** (4th S., xii., 57) a writer says:

"I bought my first steel pen from Bramah, Piccadilly, in 1825. The price was 1s. 6d. It was very thick and hard, with very little elasticity. In 1829 I read advertised in the **Times,** steel pens, with holder, 3s. per dozen, at Kendal's, in Holborn. They were hand made, and much easier to write with than Bramah's. Soon after the price fell, and steel pens became common."

In London Notes and Queries (4th S., x., 309), October 19, 1872, Mr. William Bates, speaking of a visit he paid to an old lady, at Studley (Worcestershire) about 1825, says that he saw an exquisitely-finished inkstand of pure gold, the gift of one of the Earls of Plymouth to her father, 100 years before. The inkstand was provided with a jointed gold penholder, terminating in a barrel (one slit) pen, resembling the metallic pen of the present day, except that he found that it would not write.

In "Local Notes and Queries," published in the ***Birmingham Journal and Weekly Post,*** there have appeared a number of contributions relating to the early manufacture of steel pens. We reproduce them here. A correspondent writing on June 22, 1869, says: "Daniel Fellows, of Sedgley, made steel pens about 1800."

Another writer, on the same date, says, "The first makers of steel pens were John Edwards, Hill Street, and Francis Heeley, Mount Street, Birmingham."

Respecting, the former of these, in ***Wrightson's Birmingham Directory, 1823, the following advertisement appears: "John Edwards, manufacturer of improved gold, silver, and*** elastic sleel pens, mounted in all kinds of cases, and desk handles, No. 40 Hill Street. N.B.--The pens are warranted to write exceedingly fine and free."

This advertisement contained engravings of a barrel and "nibbed" or "slip" pen.

J. Sargent, writing from Tettenhall, June 28, 1869, says:

"A journeyman blacksmith, named Fellows, of Sedgley, was the first originator of steel pens. I resided at Sedgley in 1822, when Sheldon, Fellows's apprentice, made some of these pens. He made two for me. I wrote very well with them. Sheldon himself told me that Mr. Gillott commenced making the pen from seeing some of his (Sheldon's) make."

Some one writing under the ***nom de plume*** of "Un Qui Sait," says:

"I distinctly recollect, about the year 1806, being at Fellows's home in Sedgley, and there seeing Thomas Sheldon, his apprentice, making steel pens. He knew of an entry in his books of pens bought from Fellows in 1807. He paid Sheldon L.100 in 1822. He believed Fellows made pens in 1793. Beilby and Knott (Birmingham stationers) sold these pens in considerable quantities from 1818 to 1828. Sheldon continued the trade until it was destroyed through inability to compete with the machine-made pens of Mitchell and Gillott."

Another writer, "T. S.," says:

"In 1815, an uncle of mine used to purchase these pens from Sheldon, of Sedgley. The price was eighteen shillings per dozen, ten per cent. for cash. They were barrel shape. B. Smith and Co. had in their pattern book of engravings of steel toys a drawing of one of these pens, which were sold at thirty shillings per dozen; also one in a bone handle, the top of which screwed off, for carrying in the pocket, at thirty-six shillings per dozen."

Another correspondent, writing on July 24, 1869, mentions (on authority of the late Mr. Alderman Yates) that an old man named Spittle made steel pens before any of the present makers.

In note 319 this man Spittle is mentioned by another writer, who says:

"A man named Spittle, one of the earliest makers of steel pens, lived in Chequers' Walk, Bath Row, Birmingham. He made steel pens for sale, and charged one shilling each for them. They were made with a tube to fit on a quill. I bought one from him forty-five years ago (1824)."

"E.W.," writing in 1869, says:

"In 1821 there was a B. Smith, steel toy maker, St. Paul's [Mary's] Square, Birmingham. He had a book of engravings of steel toys, among which were steel pens, made to screw on and off. This pattern book might have been one hundred years old. I sold his pens in 1823."

The Editor of "Notes and Queries" says "Smith's pattern book was probably fifty years old," and further remarks that steel pens must have been a regular article of manufacture before they appeared in a steel toy maker's pattern book.

"C.J.," in note 372, says:

"The pattern book of John Barnes, Eagle Works, Wolverhampton, contains engravings of early steel pens."

Mr. Robert Griffin says:

"In 1824 I wrote very much with a steel pen made under the direction of James Perry--a pen that lasted about eight or nine weeks, writing eight hours a day."

In note 344, "Anon" says he remembered his father (who had premises in Water Street, Birmingham), in the summer of 1823, bringing a tall, quiet, respectable man to the manufactory. He had a piece of iron, or steel, which he required to be cut up into strips of about two inches wide. The man said he was going to get the strips rolled to make into steel pens. He gave the writer of the note sixpence and a barrel pen for his trouble. In answer to inquiries the writer put to his father, the latter stated he did not know the man's name nor where he lived, but "that he met with him in a smoke room, where he (the father) sometimes spent his evenings." The writer further remarks: "Where the man had got his ideas from which induced him to try his hand at making steel pens I do not know, but I have an impression that there were several experimenters in existence at that time; and very soon afterward Mr. William (Joseph) Gillott, with whom my father was on terms of intimacy, came into notice as a maker of steel pens." This is a very important statement, as it fixes a date respecting pens being made from sheet steel.

One of the oldest toolmakers in the trade has informed us that, about the year 1823 or 1824, he was frequently taken by his father to visit an uncle named Clulee, who rented power at the Water Street mill. On these occasions his father and uncle would talk about the visits of Gillott to the latter, and the hopeful manner in which he spoke of the experiments he was then making. Gillott rented power at the Water Street mill, and was engaged in grinding and finishing penknife blades, which were inserted in one end of a silver pencil case, which his relative--Mitchell--was then making.

Now, who was this "tall, quiet, respectable man?" It could not have been Gillott, as he was not tall and the father of "Anon" knew him; and Mitchell was also a short man. We have failed to trace him, and his identity is lost among the "sowers" who failed to reap the harvest of their inventions.

Mr. George Wallis, speaking of steel pens, remarks:

"I wrote with one when a boy (1822 to 1826), having found several in a stock of old steel waste in the warehouse of a relative, a retired ornamental steel worker, at Wolverhampton. These pens were made (so I was told) for the London market, late in the last or early in the present century. Certainly they were made fifteen or, perhaps, twenty years, when I found them, as the manufactory in which they had been produced had been closed the former number of years. They consisted of a holder of steel, with flutings and facets. One was solid and tapered to lighten it; the other had a barrel with an internal screw. The pen had two screws; one was used to screw the pen into the barrel for use, and the other to secure it when turned inwards as a protection when not in use, or to carry in the pocket."

The following letter from Mr. Alderman Manton to Mr. Sam: Timmins makes us acquainted with another manufacturer of steel pens:

"THE METAL PENS OF 1823.--In a badly-constructed and unsanitary manufactory (Mr. James Collins's), at the back of 119 Suffolk Street, (Birm.), I witnessed the process of making silver and *steel* pens. As both metals were manufactured in the same manner, one description will serve. It will be remembered by a few that at that time there was a patent silver pencil case somewhat extensively manufactured, which in addition to the pencil, had a penknife, *pen* and toothpick provided. The penknife was supplied by two brothers--*Joseph and William Gillott*--who at that time rented a small shop in a corner of the yard belonging to the rolling mill of George and P.F. Muntz, Water Street, and from whose engine they obtained the small amount of steam power needed. The process of making the pens was as follows: Two narrow strips were cut from a sheet of silver or steel; they were then, by the help of the hammer and a lead cake, or piece of hard wood, curved. Afterwards the two strips were placed opposite to each other on a well-polished steel wire, and drawn through a draw-plate, the wire and plate being supplied by Wm. Billings, a celebrated tool manufacturer, occupying premises near the top of Snow Hill (Birm.). By the aid of a press, a small hole was made at a distance of half an inch or five-eighths from the end, the slit was then made by a fine saw made of watch springs. A bent pair of shears was used for cutting the end of strip into the shape of a pen; and a half-round file or smooth was used for finishing the pen. The pen was then sawn off the strip by the same saw which was used for slitting the pen. The only hardening process was the friction of the draw-plate and steel wire. I not only witnessed the process, but was a manipulator. The cost of making at that time, by a journeyman, was 2d. each; by an apprentice, about one-third of that amount. Within less than thirty years of that time, in a manufactory adjoining my own, pens were made and sold (wholesale) at 2d. per gross, and a box containing them into the bargain." (Signed) Henry Manton, September 15, 1886.

Mr. T. Vary writes that James Perry began making steel pens in Manchester, and quotes the *Saturday Magazine* to show that metallic pens were given by him as rewards of merit in schools as far back as 1819.

Mr. James Cocker, writing in the *Sheffield Daily Telegraph,* in 1869, says: "That he rolled steel wire for James Perry for penmaking in

1829."

The death of Mr. Gillott seems to have revived the discussion of the origin of steel pens, and a correspondent in the Sheffield *Daily Telegraph*, in the issue of January 11, 1872, in the following letter, puts forth a claim on behalf of a Sheffield man:

"The well-written and well-merited memoir of the late Mr. Gillott, the Birmingham steel pen maker, which has just appeared in the newspapers, affords a curious and instructive illustration of the success which not seldom attends the combined action of ingenuity, industry, shrewdness, and integrity among our labouring classes. Born in the humblest rank of our local workmen, a steady scholar in our Boys' Lancasterian School, and apprenticed to a scissors grinder, the deceased worked his way upwards into a position of influence and opulence as a manufacturer, which entitled him to take social rank with the merchant princes of the land. And if his name has long since ceased to be familiar among his once contemporary workmen in Sheffield, and is not even mentioned in the Directory, it has for several years past been recognized and respected by the visitors at the annual exhibitions of our School of Art, in connection with the many rare and valuable pictures lent by him on those occasions. The printed *fac-simile* of the autograph appeared in the 'advertising columns' of almost every newspaper in the world, and perhaps, as an expert might have said, was characteristic. In the admirable account of his life above referred to stress is laid upon one prominent and praiseworthy feature of his character, viz., his readiness to acknowledge the obscurity of his origin and the steps of his industrial success. In those details no mention is made of his Sheffield master and predecessor in the ingenious art of steel pen making. And as the notice alluded to is without dates, it is difficult to furnish information on the material point of priority, though the fact of supremacy in the trade is clear enough. In one of the columns of Lardner's Cyclopedia, published in 1833, the names of Perry, Heeley, and Skinner are mentioned as steel pen makers. With the latter, who if he did not make wealth, certainly earned a wide reputation for the low price and excellent temper of his 'steel nibs,' Mr. Gillett was a workman, in Nursery Street, Sheffield, having gone with his master from the scissors grinding stone to the making of polished steel ornaments for ladies' work, then fashionable. How much, in what way, or whether at all, he was indebted to his experience in Mr. Skinner's establishment may be questionable, but that he learnt and first saw practised in Sheffield the art that ultimately enriched him in Birmingham, he would probably be the last to deny. It is well remembered by a worthy dealer in almost every useful article, from a mouse-trap to a railroad wagon, that Gillott, soon after his establishment in Birmingham, came into our townsman's shop, and seeing on the counter a model steam engine of half-horse power, at once purchased and carried it off to give motion to some part of his pen machinery. Brass pens were made in Sheffield before the close of the last century. They mostly accompanied an 'inkpot,' called from its users an 'exciseman.' The writer of this paragraph himself made hundreds of dozens of them, which, however, be never used, nor steel ones either, as long as he could get a 'goose quill,' good, bad or indifferent. The matter of slitting the nib was kept secret by Skinner, and the double slit of Gillott more than doubled the value of his old master's invention; but a 'four-slit' pen, *i.e., with five points,* if possible to make, would be useless. The earliest experimenter in form and material was Perry, flexibility being the great desideratum; but it is curious to see how worldwide a currency Gillott's name and trade have given to the simplest shape; and still more curious to note how the makers of writing ink and paper have conformed these articles to the requirements of the uses of the steel pen. It is always gratifying, and not unprofitable, to contrast the small and feeble beginnings of any manufacturing enterprise with a large and well-merited success."

This communication appears to have caused a Mr. William Levesley to call upon the writer of the preceding epistle, and the following which appeared in the *Sheffield Daily Telegraph,* January 30, 1872, was written:

"I have to thank you for the insertion of my queries as to the early connection of Sheffield with steel pen making. In consequence of the appearance of my letter in the *Telegraph,* a cutlery manufacturer of the name of William Levesley, called upon me, and informed me that he was not only an early associate with the late Mr. Gillott, of Birmingham, but the first person who made a steel pen out of London. Stress has been laid upon Gillott's ability 'to forge and grind a knifeblade.' It is not likely he ever used the hammer on hot steel, but he was when young, and working with father, accounted an excellent penknife grinder; Skinner being a scissors grinder, and Levesley a workboard hand for the same master. A man of the name of Mitchell having married Gillott's mother, went to Birmingham, and began the cutlery business, the latter removing thither to grind for his father- in-law. His brother had also gone thither, and commenced making an article that had some run, and may be said to have united the ingenious handicrafts of Birmingham, viz., the insertion of a penknife blade at the end of a silver pencil case. Meanwhile, about the year 1825, Levesley saw a steel pen, made by Perry, of London, in Ridge's shop window, in High Street. He bought it for one shilling, and immediately set about making tools to imitate and improve upon it. He spent, he said, L.30 in not unsuccessful, though unremunerative, experiments. The flypress was at least as well known in Sheffield as in Birmingham, and its power was at once brought into requisition to work the tools for shaping, bending, and slitting the pens which were made out of sheet steel, Perry's being made out of thick wire, rolled flat, by Cocker, in Nursery Street. In 1829, Levesley was making pens for sale, and that year is said to be the earliest date of actual sales in Skinner's ledger. In 1831 he was doing a considerable business in Sheffield, and making experiments upon the article, as appears from specimens before me bearing his name. Stress has been laid upon the improvement of the double slit, introduced by Gillott, but if Levesley's statement is to be taken literally, he was the inventor of a specialty upon which, even more than on excellence of material, the merit of a steel pen is found to depend, viz., the grinding of a small hollow at the back of the nib, and about the eighth of an inch from the point. My informant described not only the beneficial action of this thinning of the metal, as well in yielding the gradual flow of the ink as in flexibility of writing, but the pleasure with which he took a specimen to Birmingham to show Gillott, and the surprise of the latter at so great and so beneficial an effect, provided by so small a cause. He at once adopted an improvement of which every pen made by him bears evidence; and when his friend visited him he told him he had fifty women employed in grinding pen points. It is pleasant to add that Gillott never visited Sheffield without calling to see his old friend Levesley, while the latter spoke of his early and later life with respect and commendation, especially in his domestic relations. It is pleasing to review a life of such humble beginnings, culminating in opulence and usefulness like that of the late Joseph Gillott, of Birmingham; nor is it less to name in connection therewith, as an early experimenter in steel pen making, our worthy townsman, William Levesley, to whose ingenious improvement every writer is so much indebted, and of whose verbal communication to me the foregoing is an imperfect sketch."

Now, in this statement, there are some dales given, but others are omitted, and that is a very unfortunate circumstance. Levesley told the writer of the article in the **Sheffield Daily Telegraph** that he made use of the fly press for working tools for shaping, bending, and slitting pens. If the writer had only given the date of this it would have been a valuable contribution toward a history of the invention. The claim of Levesley to having invented the process of grinding pens and teaching Gillott seems, to say the least, curious, because the latter was a Sheffield grinder, and the idea would certainly be quite as likely to occur to Gillott as Levesley. Besides, why did Levesley communicate the idea to Gillott in preference to Skinner, with whom he had business relations? The statement that Gillott had fifty girls employed when Levesley* called upon him on his next visit to Birmingham looks like a mistake. Fifty girls would grind on an average seven thousand gross of pens in a week, and as this correspondence appears to refer to the early part of Gillott's career, it is scarcely possible that such a number of pens were produced weekly at that period. Besides, as a matter of fact, boys were, in the first instance, employed to grind pens.

* Mr. Sam: Timmins says, "that Levesley told him that Gillott started in Birmingham as a jobbing cutler; that Mitchell had the secret of pen making; that Mitchell sent for Gillott to come to Birmingham, and that he (J.G.) first lived at the top of Water Street; that Gillott began to make pens in Bread Street; that Perry made pens from flattened steel wire, the breadth of the pen (the steel was 3s. 6d. per lb., and drawn at Old Ford); that he had seen cross grinding (at Gillott's) in Newhall Street, and fifty women at work; and that pens had double slits and cut holes. Levesley certainly knew all the Gillott family, personally, in Sheffield, and he (S. T.) had a long interview with him shortly before his death, when he mentioned all the facts given here."

Herr Ignaz Nagel, in his "Report on Writing, Drawing, and Painters' Requisites," at the Vienna Exhibition, 1873, says:

"From careful inquiries that we made in Birmingham, we learned that a knife cutler, of Sheffield, was the first man who had the idea of making pens of steel, and that a tinman of the name of Skipper [Skinner], of Sheffield, afterwards manufactured the pens in great quantities. His son developed the idea still further. This, according to our informant, was fifty years ago. A steel pen artisan, working in Birmingham, remembers perfectly well reading the announcement in a window of the High Street, in Sheffield, 1816: 'Steel pens are repaired here at sixpence apiece.' There was a man named Spittle, in Birmingham, who used to make steel pens by hand. He was succeeded by the brothers John and William Mitchell, who were manufacturers of steel pens, wholesale and by machinery, about forty- five years ago. Perry came afterwards, and took out a patent for the first steel pens, and after him Gillott, who had learnt the business with the Mitchells."

A writer in *Herbert's Encyclopoedia* published in 1837, says

"The first decided attempt to introduce metallic pens to general use was made by Mr. Wise, whose perpetual pens will doubtless be remembered by many of our readers. The name of Wise was rendered conspicuous in most of our stationers' shops some twenty-five or thirty years since, as the original inventor and general manufacturer of the steel pens."

We stated at the beginning of this article that of three men-- Mitchell, Gillott, and Mason--who might have done something toward fixing the date of the invention of manufacturing pens by the adaptation of tools worked by the screw press, only one--Mason--made a statement:

"The first making of steel pens that I know of was about the year 1780, by my late friend Mr. Harrison, for Dr. Priestley. He took sheet steel, made a tube of it, and the part joined formed the slit of the pen. He then filed away the barrel and formed the pen. I found some of the identical pens amongst other articles and used them for a long time.

"The second mode of making pens was by punching a rough blank out of thin sheet steel. This blank formed the well-known barrel pen. It was brought into the barrel shape by rounding, but before rounding it had to be filed into a better form about the nib, and when rounded in the soft state, a sharp chisel was used to mark the inside of the pen which became the slit, after hardening. Before tempering, this mark was 'tabbered' with a small hammer, and it would crack where the inside mark was made. Then it was tempered and underwent grinding, and shaping the nib until a point suitable for fine or broad, as required.

"I made barrel pens in 1828, and 'slip' pens for Perry in 1829, and the first lot of 100 at *one time* was sent November 20, 1830. Frequently, lots of 20 or 30 gross were sent between 1829 and 1830, and in 1831 I sent pens to Perry amounting to L.1421, 1s. 3d.

"Perry certainly never made a pen as they are now made, viz., the *slit cut* with press tools; all he made were *cracked* slit.

"I made steel barrel pens some time before I made 'slip' pens for Perry.

"It is doubtful when metal pens were made. The first I know of were made by Mr. Harrison, for Dr. Priestley. Perry was certainly not the first maker of steel pens, but I have no doubt that he was the first steel *slip pen* maker, and no doubt the first to use a *goose quill* for a pen holder, hence the slip pen.

"The first stick pen holders I made for Perry in 1832, and for Gillott in 1835, and sold sticks to Gillott in 1840--L.293 18s. 7d."

Mason claimed to have made barrel pens for Perry, of London, in 1828, and "slip or nibbed" pens in 1829; but he does not appear to have made any claim to priority of invention over Mitchell and Gillott.

Now, although Mitchell made no claim himself, on the death of Mr. Gillott the following letter appeared in the *Daily Post:*

"The remarks which have appeared in a local paper upon the death of Mr. J. Gillott, that the steel pen owes its existence to him, and that the adaptation of machinery to the manufacture of metallic pens was his invention, lead the public to wrong conclusions. It is due to the memory of my late father--John Mitchell--that I should state that he not only made steel pens, but used machinery in their production, for some time before Mr. Gillott commenced in that branch of business."
--HENRY MITCHELL, January 12, 1872.

In October, 1876, Mr. Henry Mitchell writes to *Aris's Gazette,* and says:

"You review, in your impression of the 23d inst., a work entitled 'British Manufacturing Industries--the Birmingham Trades,' in which the history of steel pens forms a prominent chapter. I beg to point out that my late father's name--John Mitchell--is certainly mentioned in a list of the manufacturers of the article, and, to my great surprise, simply so. In a part of the work the author states that 'The early history of steel pens is involved in obscurity.' My object in writing to you is to remove that obscurity, as I am satisfied you will be equally desirous of giving honor to whom honor is due. I claim that honor for my late father-- John Mitchell--who was the first to introduce the making of steel pens by means of tools, which were purely his own invention, and I will leave it to an enlightened public to judge if it is not one of the greatest benefits conferred on any civilized community. Whatever others may have done does not remove the fact that the inventor I have named was my father; and it is only due to him that posterity should know who originated the means whereby millions of human beings of the present time, and generations yet unborn are, and will be, enabled to communicate their thoughts to each other with a facility they otherwise would not have had. For, unless the steel pen had been manufactured by tools and machinery, that useful article would virtually be at a prohibitory price. The date of the invention I believe to be 1822 or thereabouts."

This is very emphatic; but how far may it be taken as an unprejudiced statement of facts? Well, it has never been contradicted; and Gillott never made a claim on his own behalf, as having made pens before Mitchell. Mason gave the year 1828 as the date when he commenced making pens, so that the evidence is in favor of Mitchell.

We have heard this statement of Henry Mitchell confirmed by a man who worked for Mitchell, as a boy, and who remembered pens being made for Sheldon by Mitchell. It is probable at this early period the pens were made for a few dealers, and the general public was unacquainted with the names of the manufacturers. This circumstance has no doubt contributed to involve in obscurity the early operations of Mitchell and Gillott. In a notice in *Lardner's Cyclopoedia* (written by Mr. John Holland, of Sheffield), published in 1833, the names of three penmakers only are given--Perry, Heeley, and Skinner. From this it might be supposed that there were no other penmakers at this date; but Gillott had taken out a patent in 1831, and the names of both Mitchell and Gillott appeared as penmakers in *Wrightson's Birmingham Directory* for 1830. It cannot be supposed that Mr. Holland wilfully omitted to mention the names of Mitchell and Gillott, for this writer was an impartial and painstaking collector of facts, but it is probable the notice was written some time before it was published; and, like many little masters, Mitchell and Gillot were only known as penmakers to the wholesale dealers in Birmingham, upon whom they depended for orders, consequently Mr. Holland would be ignorant of their existence.

In speaking of the demand for steel pens, the writer in Lardner's says: "The rage originated chiefly, if not altogether, in the successful speculations of Mr. James Perry, of London, whose pens, however short their merits may fall of the praise of the inventor, are certainly superior to most others composed of a like material. Perry began to make steel pens, in Manchester, in 1819, and in London in 1824." The press and tools with which these pens were made are still in the possession of Perry and Co., at their warehouse in the Holburn Viaduct. This fact tends to confirm the statement that Mr. James Perry was one of the earliest experimenters in the manufacture of the article. Levesley says he bought one of Perry's pens, which he saw in a shop window in Sheffield, in 1825, and he took it to his workshop and improved upon it. This is somewhat similar to the account given by Mason of his first experiment in pen making. Mason saw a pen of Perry's in the window of a bookseller named Peart, in Bull Street, Birmingham, in 1828, which he purchased and took home. Finding he could produce a better article, which could be sold at a cheaper rate, he made some and sent them to Mr. James Perry, in, London, and that gentleman shortly after waited upon Josiah Mason, at his place of business in Lancaster Street, and the interview resulted in Mason beginning to make pens for Perry. It will be remembered that the writer in the **Sheffield Daily Telegraph** stated that the earliest experimenter in form and material was Perry.

Leaving the honor of having originated the application of labor-saving machinery for the manufacture of steel pens to Mitchell, it would appear that the merit of having popularized the article is due to Perry. In 1830, Mr. James Perry issued a circular containing a series of engravings of metallic pens, showing the improvements he had patented in their manufacture. In this circular it is stated: "Till about six months ago the public had heard little of metallic pens. At present, it would seem that comparatively few of any other kind are in the hands of any class of the community. This sudden transition may clearly be traced to the announcement of the Patent Perryian Pens in various periodicals, about six months ago, and to the general demand which ensued for that pen in every part of the empire,"

Although this might be regarded as an ***ex-parte*** statement, it is confirmed by independent testimony that Perry popularized the article. The ***Saturday Magazine,*** 1838, says:

"About twelve years ago (1825), the celebrated Perryian pens first appeared. Mr. Perry may be regarded in the light of a great improver; many of his pens are ingenious and original in construction. He arranges his pens into ***genera*** and ***species.*** Mr. Perry first overcame the rigidity complained of in steel pens by introducing apertures between the shoulder and point of the pen, thus transferring the elasticity of the pen to a position below instead of above the shoulder. This was the subject of his patent in 1830."

Mr. Sam: Timmins, in 1866, writes:

"No skill in manufacture, however, could conquer the prejudice against any metallic pen, and to Mr. James Perry the world is much indebted for persevering advocacy of the steel pen, and for one of the most important improvements in its form. Mr. Perry, with his characteristic energy, almost forced the steel pen into use, and was supplied with pens of a first-class quality by Mr. Josiah Mason, of this town."

Furthermore, it is certain that about this time, steel pens began rapidly to supersede the use of quills,* and the trade was recognized as a rising industry. It is true that it still retained the secretive character with which its operations were conducted in its earlier days, which indeed in some respects distinguish it at the present time. Its activity or dullness seldom troubles the writers of the "Trade Reports" in the local press, although they sometimes inform their readers about good orders having been placed for mousetraps, stove screws, snuffer trays, candle extinguishers, and sad irons.

*In a humorous article, "The Web-footed Interests," which appeared in Tait's Edinburgh Magazine, vol. iii., page 280 (1833), there is a petition to the House of Commons, from Ganders, Geese & Goslings, setting forth the evils likely to ensue from the use of metallic pens. It prognosticates depression in agriculture and manufactures consequent upon a diminution in the amount of grain consumed, and a falling off in the demand for penknives; and draws an alarming picture of the possible failure of the supply of iron ware, and the total extinction of literature, likely to ensue through a stoppage in the supply of steel pens,--the web-footed interest being supposed to have ceased to exist. The petition concludes with a prayer that the manufacture of metallic pens be prohibited.

To the writers of the present generation, who can purchase fairly-good pens at one shilling or one shilling and sixpence per gross, it seems hard to realize that people once gave one shilling each for substitutes for quills. It is true that quills could then be bought for a halfpenny and penny each, but how difficult it was to acquire the art of successfully manipulating the same into a pen the following anecdote from "Edwards' Life of Rowland Hill" will testify:

"Mrs. Sinkinson, of Jamaica Row, Birmingham, tells me she went to a school in Hurst Street, and that she remembered that old Mr. Hill came one day a week to teach arithmetic, and Rowland [Sir Rowland Hill] on another to teach writing. In those days there were no steel pens, and Rowland couldn't mend a pen, so that whenever he came he was accompanied by his brother, Matthew Davenport, whose office it was to mend the pens used by the pupils the preceding week."

Sir Josiah Mason used to relate a similar circumstance in his own life, when at Kidderminster, that he accompanied his brother Richard, who was a Sunday-school teacher, to mend the pens.

Comparing the crude specimens of early steel pens with the finished productions of the present day, we may be inclined to think that some praise was due to the people who persevered in the use of them; but that the purchasers of these early productions did appreciate them we have the testimony of Mr. Robert Griffin, who says that he wrote for eight weeks, eight hours a day, with a pen made by Perry, in 1824. Now, the old *"scribes,"* as the law stationers' writers were called, were generally allowed one quill a day, and as the work of the day usually wore out the longest quill, a considerable amount of time must have been occupied in the renovation of the article.* This would be a serious inconvenience to those who could manufacture a quill into a pen, but as this was by no means an universal accomplishment, we can form an idea how even these clumsy substitutes found purchasers at such high prices.

*The writer recollects the tedious waiting for the patient usher, who from desk to desk with his penknife, mending pens, and paying very little attention to anything else; also the wonder felt and expressed at the first sight of steel nibs, and how they dug into the paper.

Tom Hood, in his "Whims and Oddities," gives some idea of the pre-steel-pen era:

"In times begone, when each man cut his quill,
    With little Perryian skill;
What horrid, awkward, bungling tools of trade
Appeared the writing instruments, home made!
What pens were sliced, hewed, hacked, and haggled out,
Slit or unslit, with many a various snout,

Aquiline, Roman, crooked, square, and snubby,
  Humpy and stubby;
Some capable of ladye-billets neat,
Some only fit for ledger-keeping clerk,
And some to grub down, Peter Stubbs, his mark,
Or smudge through some illegible receipt,
Others in florid caligraphic plans,
Equal to ships, and wiggy heads, and swans!
To try in any common inkstands then,
With all their miscellaneous stocks,
  To find a decent pen,
Was like a dip into a lucky-box;
You drew, and got one very curly,
And split like endive in some hurly-burly;
The next unslit, a square at end, a spade;
The third, incipient pop-gun, not yet made;
The fourth a broom; the fifth of no avail,
Turned upwards, like a rabbit's tail;
And last, not least, by way of a relief,
A stump that Master Richard, James, or John
Had tried his candle cookery upon,
  Making 'roast beef!'"

These early pens were at first made from a piece of steel formed into a tube, and filed into the shape of a pen by hand, the joint of the two edges forming the slit. Afterward a blank was roughly punched out, filed into shape, and the slit marked out with a chisel while the blank was in a soft state. It was then shaped, hardened, tempered, ground, and the slit cracked through by means of a hammer and tool at the place where the mark had been made. The engravings of the pens by Edwards, which appeared in **Wrightson's Directory,** 1823, seem to indicate that the piercing, side cutting and slitting were executed by mechanical appliances. Possibly, Edwards was not a manufacturer himself, but had his pens made for him by Mitchell.

In the pre-steel-pen era there were many attempts made to supersede quills. In "Peveril of the Peak," Mistress Chiffinch speaks of her *diamond pen.* There was a pen the nibs of which were of ruby, set in gold, made by Doughty. Dr. Wollaston made gold pens tipped with, rhodium.

During the time the early makers of steel pens were perfecting the article, several experimenters were offering to the public writing instruments made from various materials. Bramah patented *"quill nibs,"* made by splitting quills and cutting the semi-cylinders into sections, which were shaped into pens, and adapted to be placed in a holder. Hawkins and Mordan, in 1823, made use of horn and tortoise- shell, which was cut into "nibs," softened in water, and small pieces of ruby and other precious stones were then embedded in by pressure. In this way they insured durability and great elasticity. In order to give stability to the nib thin pieces of gold or other metal were affixed to the tortoise-shell.

Looking back at the early operations of the trade, and considering that steel pens were made by hand at the beginning of the present century, we can scarcely understand why the idea of cheapening the production by the application of labor-saving contrivances did not occur to those inventive geniuses, the proprietors of Soho. Boulton had expended some time in perfecting the manufacture of steel buttons. That local Admirable Crichton, Humphrey Jefferies, does not appear to have ever directed his attention to the manufacture of this article, which has now become a prime necessity of civilization. Yet we hear of his success in the improvement of buttons, and button-makers must have used the screw press and tools for cutting out the blank and shaping it into form; and the process of slitting had been anticipated, for printers had a brass rule-cutting machine in use, the cutters of which bore a strong resemblance to those now used for slitting steel pens. Like most of the pioneers in the path of invention, the majority of the early makers of pens were men whose business pursuits gave them no special facilities for entering upon the manufacture of steel pens. The progress of the trade from 1829 (with the exception of the period when Perry and Gillott first commenced advertising) had been gradual, but satisfactory. In one of Gillott's early advertisements, he stated that he made 490,361 gross in 1842, and 730,031 in 1843. This was an advance by leaps and bounds which has not since been maintained. Although Mason commenced making pens for Perry in the year 1828, yet it was not till 1861 that his name became known in England as a steel-pen maker. Many merchants in Birmingham and Wolverhampton, who purchased steel rings from him, had no idea that he was a maker of pens; yet on the Continent of Europe pens bearing his name were eagerly sought after. Subsequent to 1861 he was associated with Perry, until, in 1876, the trade-marks, patents, etc., were purchased by a limited liability company, who now, under the name of "Perry & Co.," have become the largest manufacturers of pens in the world.

At the present time (1889) there are thirteen firms engaged in the trade in Birmingham, and they make up about twenty-four tons of steel per week into pens and penholder tips. Making due allowance for the material used in the latter article, this consumption would probably represent a weekly average production of 200,000 grosses of pens. The Birmingham penmakers employ about 3,500 women and girls, and 650 men and boys; and besides these the number of women and girls working at making paper boxes, in which the pens are packed, would probably exceed 300. In addition to this there are several mills where steel is rolled for those firms who have not sufficient power on their own premises, but there is a difficulty in stating the number of hands employed. The wages of the females range from four shillings to fifteen shillings; those of the boys from five shillings to ten shillings. The unskilled workmen earn from twelve shillings to twenty-four shillings; and skilled men, or toolmakers, command wages varying from twenty-five shillings to three pounds. Most of the females work upon the piece-work system, but the men are paid weekly wages.

In 1835, upon the authority of a writer in the *Mechanics' Magazine,* two tons two hundred weight of steel were used weekly in the manufacture of pens. Mr. Sam: Timmins made an approximate estimate that six and a half tons of steel were used per week for steel pens in 1849, and again, in 1886, he gives the amount of steel as having increased to ten tons. It is at all times difficult to form an accurate estimate of the quantity of material used, but we believe we are within the mark in putting down the present consumption of steel at twenty-two tons weekly. From this it would appear that the trade has doubled its production during the last twenty years. Besides these Birmingham houses there are some four or five manufactories on the Continent, and two in the United States, but their productions have not increased in the same ratio as that of their English rivals. During the last twenty years a great improvement has taken place in the style of boxes and labels in which the pens are packed. Formerly (with the exception of the goods issued by Gillott and Sommerville) most of the pens were sold in boxes of the plainest description; now the covers or labels are printed in a number of colors from elaborate designs, by first-class artists, and in some cases the boxes are ornamented with well-executed portraits of royal, political, literary, or artistic celebrities. There are many peculiarities connected with the public taste as manifested in the demand for pens. The Germans use a greater variety of patterns than any other nation. The English taste is more restricted, and is generally confined to articles of the plainer shapes. Autocratic Russia and democratic America make use of the fewest patterns. By a regulation of the Imperial Government, pens in boxes, bearing portraits of the Russian royal family are prevented from entering the country, and in America public taste does not favor a demand for portrait boxes. By a law which came into operation the 1st of January, 1886, no pens can be imported into Russia bearing the name of a Russian firm. The probable purpose of this law was to encourage the establishment of a Russian manufactory. At present there are no pen works in Russia. An attempt was made in Moscow, in 1876-8, to manufacture steel pens, but the experiment proved a failure. The Germans and French are the largest buyers of first-class pens, but the Italians are content with articles of the commonest character. The chief demand for three-pointed pens comes from Spain. At present the demand for steel pens is chiefly confined to European nations and their descendants. The great Asiatic nations still write with pens made from reeds, or camel-hair pencils. A few of the natives of India and Japan, and some of the subjects of the Sultan and Khe'dive are beginning to make use of steel pens adapted to the peculiarities of their writing. From this it would appear that the possibilities of the progress of the trade in the future are very favorable; but in the meantime its productions are scattered over the globe, and even in some of the darkest corners of the earth pioneers of civilization are to be found transcribing the results of their experience with the aid of that great factor of nineteenth-century progress--an English Steel Pen.

THE MANUFACTURING PROCESSES OF STEEL PENS.

The steel from which the greater part of the metallic pens are manufactured comes from Sheffield. Notwithstanding the many names given by the venders of steel pens to the material from which they are manufactured there are but two sorts-- good and bad--and therefore Peruvian, Damascus, Amalgam, and Silver Steel are but fancy names. As a matter of fact, where a number of pre- fixes are used to describe the quality of an article it is generally found to have no claim to any of them.

The raw material is received from Sheffield in sheets six feet in length, one foot five inches in width, and 23 or 26 Birmingham wire- gauge in thickness. The first operation is the cutting of these sheets into strips of convenient width. They are then packed in an oblong iron box, placed with the open top downward in another box of the same material, and the interstices are filled up with a composition to exclude the air. The boxes are placed in a muffle, where they remain until they have gradually attained a dull red heat, and the muffle is allowed to gradually cool, or else the boxes are placed in a cooling chamber. When the boxes have been reduced to a temperature which will admit of their being handled, the contents (technically called a charge) are emptied out. Now, it will be found that the strips of steel are covered with bits of small scale, sticking to them like a loose skin, and if this were not removed before the next process--rolling--the steel, instead of being perfectly smooth, would be marked with a number of indentations, rendering it very unsightly. In order to get rid of this excrescence, the strips are immersed in a bath of diluted sulphuric acid, which loosens the scale, and are then placed in wood barrels to which broken pebbles and water are added. The barrels are kept revolving until the whole of the scaly substance has been removed and the strips have assumed a silver-gray appearance. The steel is now ready for manipulation in the rolling mill, where it is passed between successive pairs of rolls until it has been reduced to the required gauge, and this operation has to be performed with such nicety that a variation of one thousand part of an inch in the thickness of the strip would make such an alteration in the flexibility of the pens made from it as to cause considerable dissatisfaction to the purchasers of the article.

The steel on leaving the mill is conveyed to the gauging room, and it will be found to have increased to three times its original length, and now appears with a bright surface. Hitherto the operations have been conducted by men and boys; but now, in the course of manufacture, the pens will enter on a series of processes in which the quick and delicate fingers of women and girls play an important part. The strips of steel are now given out to the cutters. The *Toolmaker,* who, as a rule, both makes and sets the tools, has placed in what is known as a bolster a die, having a hole perforated through it of the exact shape of the blank to be cut; and attached to the bottom of the screwed bolt of the press is a punch, also bearing the exact shape of the blank. The girl with her left hand introduces one of the strips of steel at the back of the press, and, pulling the handle toward her with the right hand, the screw descends, driving the punch into the bed, and in so doing has perforated the strip of steel with a scissors-like cut, making a blank which falls through the opening in the die into a drawer below. Now, with her left hand she pulls the strip toward her until it is stopped by a little projection called a guide; and again the right hand moves the handle, the screw descends, and another blank is cut. The operation is continued until the whole of one side of the strip is perforated; it is then reversed and the other side treated in a similar way. If you were to hold up the strip thus manipulated--now called scrap--you would find that in some particular part the perforations approach so nearly to each other as to form a slight bar, which breaks easily between the thumb and finger. This is rendered necessary from the fact that steel scrap is worth only one-fifth of the value of the raw material, and, as under the most favorable conditions, the scrap averages one-third the original weight given out for cutting, it behooves the manufacturer to reduce the scrap as much as practicable. If these blanks are examined, a small V-shaped indentation, looking like a defect, will be found upon the upper edge of that part inserted in the holder. This small mark plays an important part in the succeeding processes. To a casual observer there does not appear much difference between the two sides of the blank; but, however well the tools are made, that side of the blank which is uppermost in cutting out will be rougher than the under side. This mark enables the operator to distinguish at a glance the smooth side, and by always keeping the rough side upward the burr is polished off in a later process. The blanks are now ready to be passed to the next process-- *marking.* This operation is performed by a female, with the aid of a stamp. The precise mark required is cut upon a piece of steel, and, being placed in the hammer of the stamp, the girl puts her right foot into a stirrup attached to a rope, which is passed round a pulley, and, pressing downward, causes the hammer to ascend. Taking a handful of blanks with her left hand, by a dexterous motion she makes a little train of them between the thumb and finger in parallel order, presenting the first in the most ready position to be passed to the other hand. The right hand is brought toward the left, and, taking a blank, places it with the point toward the worker in a guide upon the bed of the stamp, then by suddenly letting the hammer descend a blow is struck upon the blank, which gives an impression of the name cut upon the punch. The quick fingers of the operator pass backward and forward with such rapidity that a skillful girl will mark from two hundred to two hundred and fifty gross per day. If the mark required is unusually large, the marking process is deferred until after the pen has been pierced, in order that the blank may be annealed (or softened), which takes the impression more readily than the hard steel.

Now, in order to make a metallic pen suitable for writing it is necessary to consider some means of producing elasticity, and also to devise some method by which the smooth steel shall cause the ink to attach itself to the pen. This is brought about by the next process-- *piercing*. In this operation the tools are of a very delicate character, and as the center pierce (the aperture in which the slit terminates) is frequently of an ornamental design the tools, being small, have to be made with great precision. The piercing punch and bed having been fixed in a screw press, and an ingenious arrangement of guides fastened thereto, the girl selects a blank from a tray on her left hand, and, placing it in its proper position by the aid of the guides, pushes the fly of the press from her, the screw descends, driving the punch into the bed, and the operation of piercing is completed.

The blanks are still moderately hard, and before they can be made to take the shape of a pen it is necessary that they should be softened, which is effected by the process called *annealing.* The blanks having been freed from the dust and garbase that has become attached to them are carefully placed in round iron pots, which are again inclosed in larger ones and covered over with charcoal dust to prevent the entrance of gases, and put into the muffle, heated to a dull red, and then allowed to cool.

The blanks are now soft and pliable, readily taking the various shapes into which pens are made by the next process, called *raising.* This operation is performed by the aid of a punch and die fitted into a screw-press. The punch is fitted into a contrivance called a false nose, fixed in the bottom of the screw of the press; and the die or bed is placed in a cylindrical piece of steel (called a bolster) with a groove cut for the reception of the die, the bolster being fastened to the bottom of the press by a screw underneath. The punch and die being fixed so as to exactly fit each other, the toolmaker places a small piece of tissue paper between them, takes an impression, examines it, and proceeds to rectify any inequality in the pressure, so as to insure perfection in the shape. This being accomplished, the toolmaker fixes four pieces of steel (called guides) to the bolster in such positions that the operator is enabled to slide the blank into the bed, where it is held by the guides till the punch descends, forces the blank into the bed, and gives the pen its shape. The article is now narrower than it was in its blank form, and the girl pushes it through the tools with a small stick held in the hand with which she works the press handle, while with the other hand she places another blank in its position in the bed.

The pen is now shaped or raised, but it is still soft, and consequently another process is necessitated-- *hardening.* This is effected by placing the pens in thin layers in round pans with lids. They are placed in the muffle for a period varying from twenty to thirty minutes, during which time they have acquired a bright red heat. The workman then withdraws them and empties the contents into a large bucket immersed in a tank of oil. The bucket is perforated at the bottom, and being elevated, the oil drains off. The pens are next placed in a perforated cylinder, which, being set in motion, revolves and drains off the remainder of the oil. The pens are still greasy, and as brittle as glass; and in order to free them from the grease they are again placed in perforated buckets and immersed in a tank of boiling soda water. After they are freed from the grease the pens are put into an iron cylinder, which is kept revolving over a charcoal fire until they are softened or tempered down to the special degree required. In this process the workman is guided by the color, which indicates the varying temperature of the metal of which the articles are made. Brittleness has given place to pliability, but the pens are black in color and scratch at the point, and to remedy this defect they are subjected to the next process-- *scouring.* In order to do this the pens are dipped in a bath of diluted sulphuric acid--called pickle-- which frees the articles from any extraneous substances they may have acquired in the hardening and tempering processes. This requires to be done with great care, or the acid would injure the steel. The pens are then placed in iron barrels with a quantity of water and small pebbly-looking material. This latter material is composed of annealing pots broken and ground fine enough to pass readily through a fine riddle. The barrel being set in motion, the pens are scoured for periods varying from five to eight hours, and are placed again in barrels with dry pot for about the same period, after which they are put into other barrels together with a quantity of dry sawdust. On being taken out of these barrels the body of the pen has acquired a bright silver color, and the point has been rounded.

The article has now the shape and appearance of a finished pen, and yet it possesses none of its characteristics, and, if tried, will be found to have no more action than a lead pencil, as it is deficient in that important part of a writing instrument--the slit. Before being slit the pen is ground between the centre pierce and the point. This process is performed by girls, with the aid of what is called a "bob" or "glazer." The "bob" is a circular piece of alder wood about ten and a half inches in diameter and half an inch in width. Round this a piece of leather is stretched and dressed with emery. A spindle is driven through the centre, and the two ends placed in sockets. The "bob" is set in motion by means of a leather band, and the girl holding a pen firmly, with a light touch grinds off a portion of the surface.

This operation being completed, the last and most important mechanical operation has to be performed-- *slitting.* The tools with which this process is effected are two oblong pieces of steel about an inch and a half long, three-eighths of an inch thick, and an inch and a quarter wide. These are called the cutters, and upon the preparation and setting of these the successful issue of the process depends. The edges of these cutters are equal in delicacy to the cutting edge of a razor, but the shape is more suggestive of a portion cut from the thickest part of a large pair of shears. The cutter being fixed in the press, a pair of guides are screwed on either side, and a small tool called a table, or rest, being attached to the contrivance called a bolster, which holds the bottom cutter, the operator takes a pen, places it on the table, pushes the point up toward the guide, pulls the handle, the upper cutter descends, meets the lower one, and the process of slitting is completed.

Now, although this operation completes the mechanical processes of pen making, the article is by no means finished. If you examine the pen now you will find that the outer edge of each point is smooth, while the inside edges which have just been made by the slit are sharp and scratch. To remove this defect the operation of "barreling" has to be again resorted to. The pens are again placed in the iron barrels with pounded pot, kept revolving from five to six hours, and finally polished in sawdust.

The pens are now of a bright silver-steel color and perfectly smooth, but as they are required in various tints, they are colored and afterward varnished to prevent rust. To accomplish the first of these results the articles are placed in a copper or iron cylinder and kept revolving over a coke fire until the requisite tint is obtained, the color depending upon the temperature of the cylinder. If the pens are intended to be lacquered they are placed in a solution of shellac dissolved in methylated spirits. The spirit is drained off, and the pens are placed in wire cylinders and kept revolving until the action of the air dries the lacquer. They are then scattered upon iron trays, inserted in an oven, and the heat diffuses the lacquer equally over the surface of the pens, so that when they have cooled down they have a glossy appearance, which gives to them an air of finish and prevents rust.

The pen is now finished as far as manufacturing processes are concerned, yet before it can be offered to the public it has to undergo a rigid examination called *"looking over."* This is performed by trained girls, and when the defective ones have been sorted out the good pens are sent to the finished warehouse to be put up into boxes. These boxes are of various descriptions, adapted to suit the markets for which they are intended. In many instances the labels which form the covers of the boxes are elaborately printed from first-class designs, and some of them have highly-finished steel engravings of royal personages and celebrities in the scientific, literary, musical, and political world. The quantities contained in these boxes vary with the countries for which they are intended; for the manufacturers study the wants of their customers, and do not offer articles counted in dozens to people who reckon by tens.

We have now traced the manufacture of this little article from its beginning as a plain piece of steel through all its stages until it has developed into that indispensable requisite of daily life--a pen.

HISTORY OF THE PERRYIAN PEN WORKS.

The firm of Messrs. Perry & Co., London, was founded in the year 1824 by Mr. James Perry, who carried on business originally in Manchester, then in London. Mr. James Perry died in the year 1843. Mr. Stephen Perry, who conducted the business afterward in partnership with Mr. Hayes and others, died in the year 1873, and was succeeded by his sons, Messrs. Joseph John and Lewis Henry Perry. The firm of Perry & Co. was known all over Europe as the house which first introduced to the commercial world steel pens of a superior quality, and in many countries steel pens are now known under the general denomination of *"Perry pens."* The first pens were manufactured by Perry & Co. in London, principally from flattened or ribbon steel wire, and in the year 1828 Mr. Josiah, afterward Sir Josiah, Mason, ***then a manufacturer of steel split rings,*** produced steel pens so much superior to the pens made up to that period that Messrs. Perry & Co. entered into contracts with him for the sole supply of all the pens they might require; this connection continued up to the time of the formation of this company. In the meantime, Messrs. Perry & Co. had also introduced the sale of elastic bands and pencil cases; the production of the latter was confided to Mr. W.E. Wiley, who, in the year 1850, began the manufacture first of gold pens, afterward of pencil cases. Messrs. Perry & Co. also contracted with Mr. Wiley for the purchase of all the pencil cases they might dispose of, and thus Mr. Wiley's works assumed gigantic proportions. Mr. Alfred Sommerville, who had been connected with the steel-pen trade since its infancy, established the firm of A. Sommerville & Co. in the year 1851. Although he, in the year 1857, began manufacturing steel pens in connection with a partner, he likewise contracted with Mr. Josiah Mason for a superior class of steel pens, principally intended for the Continental markets, and many of which were either his own invention or suggested by him. Mr. Sommerville desiring to retire from business, Sir Josiah Mason purchased his trade in the year 1870, but continued to carry it on under the old style of A. Sommerville & Co. These four businesses being so intimately connected and dependent upon each other, some gentlemen of eminence in the manufacturing town of Birmingham decided, in conjunction with some of the leading proprietors, to establish a limited company, for the purpose of uniting and amalgamating inseparably the various establishments, and thus the company of *"Perry & Co., Limited,"* was formed.

On the spot forming the principal entrance to the works, Mr. Samuel Harrison, in the year 1778, founded a manufactory in which he carried on his invention of steel split rings; but Mr. Harrison, who was an ingenious mechanic, also manufactured mathematical instruments, some of which were used by Dr. Priestley in his researches, and on one occasion he made a steel pen for Dr. Priestley, probably the first steel pen ever produced. Mr. Josiah Mason succeeded to the business of Mr. Harrison in 1823, and in 1828 began the manufacture of steel pens. For several years he gave his whole attention to improvements in the manufacture of steel pens, and Mr. Perry took out several most important patents for the improvement of steel pens, many of which have not been surpassed in ingenuity or in utility, and the principal among them, the so-called "double patent," is universally applied by the pen trade to a great number of pens to this very day. In 1842 Mr. Mason's attention was absorbed by the process of electroplating and gilding, at that time invented and carried on by Mr. Elkington, in partnership with whom he founded the great firm of Elkington, Mason & Co. For some years the production of pens flagged, but in 1852 a nephew of Sir Josiah Mason, Mr. Isaac Smith (deceased in 1868), gave a new stimulus to the manufacture of pens, and from that time the production gradually increased until it assumed its present proportions. The manufactory now covers nearly two acres; it occupies a whole square and fronts four streets. In the building fronting Lancaster Street (five stories high) the offices, warehouses and storerooms of finished goods are distributed. The underground floor forms a huge machine shop, in which all the presses, rolls, and general iron and machine work employed throughout the manufactory are produced by skillful mechanics. Behind the front building there are several courtyards and quadrangles, in the largest of which are placed in a row five double-flue boilers, each 20 feet long by 7 feet diameter, working at a pressure of more than 55 lb. to the square inch, supplying the steam power both for propelling the steam engines and for heating the manufactory. In the rolling mill, measuing 64 by 38 feet, three double-cylinder engines, working up to 293 indicated horse-power, give motion to 18 pairs of rolls, rolling four to six tons of steel per week. The largest workshops are the slitting and grinding rooms, 64 by 38 feet, the latter 24 feet high. In the slitting room 90 girls apply the last mechanical process to the manufacture of steel pens, in slitting them by presses of ingenious construction. In the grinding room more than 160 girls are busily employed cross and straight grinding steel pens on wood cylinders covered with emery. The room in which the finished pens are placed in boxes measures 54 by 30 feet, and in it alone are employed 50 girls boxing and labeling steel pens, or fitting penholder tips on handles of various materials, principally of cedar. In that part of the building having a frontage on Corporation Street there is a dining room 86 feet 6 inches long by 68 feet wide, fitted up with tables to accommodate 600 people. Here the employees are served with a warm dinner at prices varying from 2d. to 6d. At one end of the room there is a stage, where dramatic entertainments and concerts are given in the winter season by the workpeople. At the other end there is a library, in a glazed partition, containing about 2,000 volumes of standard works. These books are issued to the hands employed by the firm free. One of the important features of this manufactory is the employment of muffles heated by gas produced from Siemens's gas generators. These muffles allow the heat to be regulated to a nicety, and enable the company to carry on the process of annealing and hardening to very great perfection.

The manufacture of steel pens employs in all about 900 workpeople, the weekly production is 45,000 gross, which quantity will shortly be increased to 50,000 gross, per week. Six smaller steam engines are employed independently of those already mentioned in various parts of the works. The manufacture of penholder sticks is carried on in two separate buildings. Penholder sticks were produced by Mr. Mason as far back as 1835, but their manufacture had lapsed; it was only resumed eight years ago, since which time, by new and ingenious machinery, principally the inventions of Mr. W. E. Wiley, the managing director, it has assumed proportions of great magnitude.

The pencil case and solitaire works carried on by Mr. Wiley, first alone, and then in co-partnership with his son in Graham Street, have now been transferred to Lancaster Street.

Pencil cases, first introduced by Messrs. Mordan & Lund, in London, have undergone various changes and improvements, the principal of which was a lead holder passing through the point of the pencil case, which was slit for that purpose. This invention was patented by Mr. Wiley in the year 1857, and created a complete revolution in the pencil-case trade, as it enabled the manufacturers to use a thicker and longer lead, which could be propelled and withdrawn at will and would last in daily use more than six months. This patented mechanism was introduced into cases made from hard wood, bone and ivory, but since the year 1868 a composition called aluminium gold, so resembling gold that it cannot be distinguished from it, and resisting the effects of oxidation, consequently free from tarnish, made a further revolution in the pencil-case trade, enabling the million to possess an elegant and highly-wrought pencil case at a very moderate price. Messrs. Perry & Co., of London, gave to this manufacture publicity in every part of Europe, and the quantities produced and sold are incredible.

In 1874 a new patent was added to the many inventions for which this establishment was famous. Its purpose was to produce a solitaire stud made in two parts, so as to enable its ready application without the trouble of passing a button of large diameter through a small buttonhole. A self-acting steel spring is fixed in the upper part of the stud, and snaps as soon as inserted into the lower part, where a slight pressure on two projections releases the springs and permits the separation of the two parts. These solitaires are manufactured of gold, silver, and a variety of other metals, the principal of which is gold plate. There are now more than five hundred patterns in existence, and this useful manufacture grows daily in extension. Perry & Co.'s paper binders, an article now universally used for fastening together loose papers, cloth patterns, etc., are produced in infinite styles and sizes, principally by self-acting machinery.

The total number of workpeople employed in the company's manufactories exceeds 1,300.

The business of Perry & Co. was carried on for more than forty years at 37 Red Lion Square, London, but the increase of business and the reconstruction of London required that a more central position should be found for the development of the commercial department of the company. Large and handsome warehouses having been constructed on the Holborn Viaduct, the company transferred their London depot to a building five stories high on the side fronting the Holborn Viaduct and eight stories high at the back. In this immense warehouse are stored not only the produce of the manufactories of this company, but also special articles for which this firm has been famous for the last thirty years, principally the elastic or endless bands, patented by Mr. Daft and Mr. Stephen Perry, and originally introduced by Perry & Co. in conjunction with McIntosh & Co., afterward in conjunction with Warne & Co. Perry's Royal Aromatic Bands are now an indispensable article, and may be procured in every city of the world. Every fancy article required by stationers can be found in these vast stores. An illustrated price current which appears monthly, and which numbers more than 120 pages, gives fair idea of the variety of articles of which samples and stock can be found ready for daily delivery. The increase of business has been so rapid that the company found it necessary to lease the adjoining premises, which is stored with some of the two thousand articles forming the staple trade of the London depot, and the principal of which are the following: American Letter Files, Clips (now manufactured in Lancaster Street), Marking and other Inks, Aromatic Bands, Audascript Pens, Bostonite Goods, Cigar Lighters, Copying Ink and Copying Ink Powder, Copying Ink Pencils, Copying Presses, Corrugated Imperial Bands, Essence of Ink, Grease Extractors, India Rubber for Erasing, Ink and Pencil Erasers, Ink Extractors, Patent and other Inkstands in every variety, Key Rings, Letter Clips, Letter Files, Metallic Books, Paper Binders, Pencil Point Protectors, Pencils and Pencil Cases, Penholders, Pen Knives, Pen Racks, Gold Pens, Portfolios, Presses, Scotch Tartan Fancy Goods, Solitaires or Sleeve Links, etc., etc., etc.

This establishment is under the exclusive management of Mr. Joseph J. Perry, managing director.

[The illustrations in this work are engraved from pen-and-ink sketches executed by Walter Langley with a Perry's No. 25 pen.]

The Codes Of Hammurabi And Moses
W. W. Davies

QTY

The discovery of the Hammurabi Code is one of the greatest achievements of archaeology, and is of paramount interest, not only to the student of the Bible, but also to all those interested in ancient history...

Religion   **ISBN:** *1-59462-338-4*   **Pages:132**
MSRP $12.95

The Theory of Moral Sentiments
Adam Smith

QTY

This work from 1749. contains original theories of conscience amd moral judgment and it is the foundation for systemof morals.

Philosophy **ISBN:** *1-59462-777-0*   **Pages:536**
MSRP $19.95

Jessica's First Prayer
Hesba Stretton

QTY

In a screened and secluded corner of one of the many railway-bridges which span the streets of London there could be seen a few years ago, from five o'clock every morning until half past eight, a tidily set-out coffee-stall, consisting of a trestle and board, upon which stood two large tin cans, with a small fire of charcoal burning under each so as to keep the coffee boiling during the early hours of the morning when the work-people were thronging into the city on their way to their daily toil...

Pages:84

Childrens   **ISBN:** *1-59462-373-2*   *MSRP $9.95*

My Life and Work
Henry Ford

QTY

Henry Ford revolutionized the world with his implementation of mass production for the Model T automobile. Gain valuable business insight into his life and work with his own auto-biography... "We have only started on our development of our country we have not as yet, with all our talk of wonderful progress, done more than scratch the surface. The progress has been wonderful enough but..."

Pages:300

Biographies/ **ISBN:** *1-59462-198-5*   *MSRP $21.95*

The Art of Cross-Examination
Francis Wellman

QTY

I presume it is the experience of every author, after his first book is published upon an important subject, to be almost overwhelmed with a wealth of ideas and illustrations which could readily have been included in his book, and which to his own mind, at least, seem to make a second edition inevitable. Such certainly was the case with me; and when the first edition had reached its sixth impression in five months, I rejoiced to learn that it seemed to my publishers that the book had met with a sufficiently favorable reception to justify a second and considerably enlarged edition. ...

Pages:412

Reference   **ISBN:** *1-59462-647-2*   *MSRP $19.95*

On the Duty of Civil Disobedience
Henry David Thoreau

QTY

Thoreau wrote his famous essay, On the Duty of Civil Disobedience, as a protest against an unjust but popular war and the immoral but popular institution of slave-owning. He did more than write—he declined to pay his taxes, and was hauled off to gaol in consequence. Who can say how much this refusal of his hastened the end of the war and of slavery ?

Law   **ISBN:** *1-59462-747-9*   **Pages:48**

MSRP $7.45

Dream Psychology Psychoanalysis for Beginners
Sigmund Freud

QTY

Sigmund Freud, born Sigismund Schlomo Freud (May 6, 1856 - September 23, 1939), was a Jewish-Austrian neurologist and psychiatrist who co-founded the psychoanalytic school of psychology. Freud is best known for his theories of the unconscious mind, especially involving the mechanism of repression; his redefinition of sexual desire as mobile and directed towards a wide variety of objects; and his therapeutic techniques, especially his understanding of transference in the therapeutic relationship and the presumed value of dreams as sources of insight into unconscious desires.

Pages:196

Psychology   **ISBN:** *1-59462-905-6*   *MSRP $15.45*

The Miracle of Right Thought
Orison Swett Marden

QTY

Believe with all of your heart that you will do what you were made to do. When the mind has once formed the habit of holding cheerful, happy, prosperous pictures, it will not be easy to form the opposite habit. It does not matter how improbable or how far away this realization may see, or how dark the prospects may be, if we visualize them as best we can, as vividly as possible, hold tenaciously to them and vigorously struggle to attain them, they will gradually become actualized, realized in the life. But a desire, a longing without endeavor, a yearning abandoned or held indifferently will vanish without realization.

Pages:360

Self Help   **ISBN:** *1-59462-644-8*   *MSRP $25.45*

The Rosicrucian Cosmo-Conception Mystic Christianity *by Max Heindel* ISBN: *1-59462-188-8* **$38.95**
The Rosicrucian Cosmo-conception is not dogmatic, neither does it appeal to any other authority than the reason of the student. It is: not controversial, but is: sent forth in the, hope that it may help to clear... New Age/Religion Pages 646

Abandonment To Divine Providence *by Jean-Pierre de Caussade* ISBN: *1-59462-228-0* **$25.95**
"The Rev. Jean Pierre de Caussade was one of the most remarkable spiritual writers of the Society of Jesus in France in the 18th Century. His death took place at Toulouse in 1751. His works have gone through many editions and have been republished... Inspirational/Religion Pages 400

Mental Chemistry *by Charles Haanel* ISBN: *1-59462-192-6* **$23.95**
Mental Chemistry allows the change of material conditions by combining and appropriately utilizing the power of the mind. Much like applied chemistry creates something new and unique out of careful combinations of chemicals the mastery of mental chemistry... New Age Pages 354

The Letters of Robert Browning and Elizabeth Barret Barrett 1845-1846 vol II ISBN: *1-59462-193-4* **$35.95**
by Robert Browning and Elizabeth Barrett Biographies Pages 596

Gleanings In Genesis (volume I) *by Arthur W. Pink* ISBN: *1-59462-130-6* **$27.45**
Appropriately has Genesis been termed "the seed plot of the Bible" for in it we have, in germ form, almost all of the great doctrines which are afterwards fully developed in the books of Scripture which follow... Religion/Inspirational Pages 420

The Master Key *by L. W. de Laurence* ISBN: *1-59462-001-6* **$30.95**
In no branch of human knowledge has there been a more lively increase of the spirit of research during the past few years than in the study of Psychology, Concentration and Mental Discipline. The requests for authentic lessons in Thought Control, Mental Discipline and... New Age/Business Pages 422

The Lesser Key Of Solomon Goetia *by L. W. de Laurence* ISBN: *1-59462-092-X* **$9.95**
This translation of the first book of the "Lemegton" is now for the first time made accessible to students of Talismanic Magic was done, after careful collation and edition, from numerous Ancient Manuscripts in Hebrew, Latin, and French... New Age/Occult Pages 92

Rubaiyat Of Omar Khayyam *by Edward Fitzgerald* ISBN:*1-59462-332-5* **$13.95**
Edward Fitzgerald, whom the world has already learned, in spite of his own efforts to remain within the shadow of anonymity, to look upon as one of the rarest poets of the century, was born at Bredfield, in Suffolk, on the 31st of March, 1809. He was the third son of John Purcell... Music Pages 172

Ancient Law *by Henry Maine* ISBN: *1-59462-128-4* **$29.95**
The chief object of the following pages is to indicate some of the earliest ideas of mankind, as they are reflected in Ancient Law, and to point out the relation of those ideas to modern thought. Religiom/History Pages 452

Far-Away Stories *by William J. Locke* ISBN: *1-59462-129-2* **$19.45**
"Good wine needs no bush, but a collection of mixed vintages does. And this book is just such a collection. Some of the stories I do not want to remain buried for ever in the museum files of dead magazine-numbers an author's not unpardonable vanity..." Fiction Pages 272

Life of David Crockett *by David Crockett* ISBN: *1-59462-250-7* **$27.45**
"Colonel David Crockett was one of the most remarkable men of the times in which he lived. Born in humble life, but gifted with a strong will, an indomitable courage, and unremitting perseverance... Biographies/New Age Pages 424

Lip-Reading *by Edward Nitchie* ISBN: *1-59462-206-X* **$25.95**
Edward B. Nitchie, founder of the New York School for the Hard of Hearing, now the Nitchie School of Lip-Reading, Inc, wrote "LIP-READING Principles and Practice". The development and perfecting of this meritorious work on lip-reading was an undertaking... How-to Pages 400

A Handbook of Suggestive Therapeutics, Applied Hypnotism, Psychic Science ISBN: *1-59462-214-0* **$24.95**
by Henry Munro Health/New Age/Health/Self-help Pages 376

A Doll's House: and Two Other Plays *by Henrik Ibsen* ISBN: *1-59462-112-8* **$19.95**
Henrik Ibsen created this classic when in revolutionary 1848 Rome. Introducing some striking concepts in playwriting for the realist genre, this play has been studied the world over. Fiction/Classics/Plays 308

The Light of Asia *by sir Edwin Arnold* ISBN: *1-59462-204-3* **$13.95**
In this poetic masterpiece, Edwin Arnold describes the life and teachings of Buddha. The man who was to become known as Buddha to the world was born as Prince Gautama of India but he rejected the worldly riches and abandoned the reigns of power when... Religion/History/Biographies Pages 170

The Complete Works of Guy de Maupassant *by Guy de Maupassant* ISBN: *1-59462-157-8* **$16.95**
"For days and days, nights and nights, I had dreamed of that first kiss which was to consecrate our engagement, and I knew not on what spot I should put my lips..." Fiction/Classics Pages 240

The Art of Cross-Examination *by Francis L. Wellman* ISBN: *1-59462-309-0* **$26.95**
Written by a renowned trial lawyer, Wellman imparts his experience and uses case studies to explain how to use psychology to extract desired information through questioning. How-to/Science/Reference Pages 408

Answered or Unanswered? *by Louisa Vaughan* ISBN: *1-59462-248-5* **$10.95**
Miracles of Faith in China Religion Pages 112

The Edinburgh Lectures on Mental Science (1909) *by Thomas* ISBN: *1-59462-008-3* **$11.95**
This book contains the substance of a course of lectures recently given by the writer in the Queen Street Hail, Edinburgh. Its purpose is to indicate the Natural Principles governing the relation between Mental Action and Material Conditions... New Age/Psychology Pages 148

Ayesha *by H. Rider Haggard* ISBN: *1-59462-301-5* **$24.95**
Verily and indeed it is the unexpected that happens! Probably if there was one person upon the earth from whom the Editor of this, and of a certain previous history, did not expect to hear again... Classics Pages 380

Ayala's Angel *by Anthony Trollope* ISBN: *1-59462-352-X* **$29.95**
The two girls were both pretty, but Lucy who was twenty-one who supposed to be simple and comparatively unattractive, whereas Ayala was credited, as her Bombwhat romantic might show, with poetic charm and a taste for romance. Ayala when her father died was nineteen... Fiction Pages 484

The American Commonwealth *by James Bryce* ISBN: *1-59462-286-8* **$34.45**
An interpretation of American democratic political theory. It examines political mechanics and society from the perspective of Scotsman James Bryce Politics Pages 572

Stories of the Pilgrims *by Margaret P. Pumphrey* ISBN: *1-59462-116-0* **$17.95**
This book explores pilgrims religious oppression in England as well as their escape to Holland and eventual crossing to America on the Mayflower, and their early days in New England... History Pages 268

QTY

The Fasting Cure *by Sinclair Upton*   ISBN: *1-59462-222-1*   **$13.95**
In the Cosmopolitan Magazine for May, 1910, and in the Contemporary Review (London) for April, 1910, I published an article dealing with my experiences in fasting. I have written a great many magazine articles, but never one which attracted so much attention...   New Age/Self Help/Health Pages 164

Hebrew Astrology *by Sepharial*   ISBN: *1-59462-308-2*   **$13.45**
In these days of advanced thinking it is a matter of common observation that we have left many of the old landmarks behind and that we are now pressing forward to greater heights and to a wider horizon than that which represented the mind-content of our progenitors...   Astrology Pages 144

Thought Vibration or The Law of Attraction in the Thought World   ISBN: *1-59462-127-6*   **$12.95**
by William Walker Atkinson   Psychology/Religion Pages 144

Optimism *by Helen Keller*   ISBN: *1-59462-108-X*   **$15.95**
Helen Keller was blind, deaf, and mute since 19 months old, yet famously learned how to overcome these handicaps, communicate with the world, and spread her lectures promoting optimism. An inspiring read for everyone...   Biographies/Inspirational Pages 84

Sara Crewe *by Frances Burnett*   ISBN: *1-59462-360-0*   **$9.45**
In the first place, Miss Minchin lived in London. Her home was a large, dull, tall one, in a large, dull square, where all the houses were alike, and all the sparrows were alike, and where all the door-knockers made the same heavy sound...   Childrens/Classic Pages 88

The Autobiography of Benjamin Franklin *by Benjamin Franklin*   ISBN: *1-59462-135-7*   **$24.95**
The Autobiography of Benjamin Franklin has probably been more extensively read than any other American historical work, and no other book of its kind has had such ups and downs of fortune. Franklin lived for many years in England, where he was agent...   Biographies/History Pages 332

Name	
Email	
Telephone	
Address	
City, State ZIP	

☐ **Credit Card**   ☐ **Check / Money Order**

Credit Card Number	
Expiration Date	
Signature	

Please Mail to: Book Jungle
PO Box 2226
Champaign, IL 61825
or Fax to: 630-214-0564

ORDERING INFORMATION

web: *www.bookjungle.com*
email: *sales@bookjungle.com*
fax: *630-214-0564*
mail: *Book Jungle PO Box 2226 Champaign, IL 61825*
or PayPal *to sales@bookjungle.com*

Please contact us for bulk discounts

DIRECT-ORDER TERMS

**20% Discount if You Order
Two or More Books**
Free Domestic Shipping!
Accepted: Master Card, Visa,
Discover, American Express